RAINBOW magic

The Weather Fairies

For Jean, with love and thanks for
the many pearls of wisdom!

Special thanks to
Narinder Dhami

ORCHARD BOOKS
96 Leonard Street, London EC2A 4XD
Orchard Books Australia
32/45-51 Huntley Street, Alexandria, NSW 2015
A Paperback Original
First published in Great Britain in 2004
Rainbow Magic is a registered trademark of Working Partners Limited
Series created by Working Partners Limited, London W6 0QT
Text © Working Partners Limited 2004
Illustrations © Georgie Ripper 2004
The right of Georgie Ripper to be identified as the illustrator
of this work has been asserted by her in accordance
with the Copyright, Designs and Patents Act, 1988.
A CIP catalogue record for this book is available
from the British Library.
ISBN 1 84362 635 7
9 10
Printed in China

Pearl the Cloud Fairy

by Daisy Meadows

illustrated by Georgie Ripper

ORCHARD BOOKS

The
Fairyland
Palace

Forest

Sweet Factory

The
Village
Hall

River

Wetherbury Village

Goblins green and goblins small,
I cast this spell to make you tall.
As high as the palace you shall grow.
My icy magic makes it so.

Then steal Doodle's magic feathers,
Used by the fairies to make all weathers.
Climate chaos I have planned
On Earth, and here, in Fairyland!

Contents

Missing Fidget

"What's the weather like today, Kirsty?" asked Rachel Walker eagerly. She pushed back the duvet. "Do you think there's magic in the air?"

Kirsty Tate was standing at the bedroom window, staring out over the garden. "It seems like an ordinary day," she sighed, a disappointed look on her face.

"The sky's grey and cloudy."

"Never mind." Rachel jumped out of bed, and went to join her friend. "Remember what Titania, the Fairy Queen, told us. Don't look too hard for magic—"

"Because the magic will find you!" Kirsty finished with a smile.

Rachel and Kirsty were good friends who shared a very special secret. They were best friends with the fairies! When Jack Frost had put a spell on the seven Rainbow Fairies, scattering them far and wide, Rachel and Kirsty had helped them to return to Fairyland. Now Jack Frost was up to mischief again – this time with the Weather Fairies. And once more, the Fairy King and Queen had called on Rachel and Kirsty for help.

"Look at Doodle." Rachel pointed at the cockerel weather-vane, which sat on top of the old barn. "Don't you think he looks a bit happier, now that he's got two of his tail feathers back?"

Kirsty nodded. "Let's hope we find all his feathers before you go home," she replied. "Then the weather in Fairyland can get back to normal again!"

With his seven magic tail feathers and the help of the Weather Fairies, Doodle the cockerel controlled Fairyland's weather. But Jack Frost had sent his mean goblin servants to steal poor Doodle's feathers. Doodle chased the goblin thieves into the human world – but without his magic, and away from Fairyland, he found himself transformed into an ordinary, rusty weather-vane!

Kirsty's dad had found him lying in the park, and brought him home to put him on the roof of the barn – never realising what a magical creature Doodle really was!

Meanwhile, the weather in Fairyland was in a terrible muddle – and it would remain so until Rachel and Kirsty could give Doodle all his feathers back and send him home.

"Well, we've made a good start," said Rachel, beginning to dress. "With the help of Crystal the Snow Fairy, and Abigail the Breeze Fairy, we've already found two feathers!"

The King and Queen had promised Kirsty and Rachel that each of the seven Weather Fairies would come to help them, whenever they were needed.

"Girls, are you awake?" Kirsty's mum called from downstairs. "Breakfast's ready."

"Coming," Kirsty shouted back.

"I wish we knew what Doodle was trying to tell us yesterday," said Rachel, as she and Kirsty clattered downstairs. Each time one of Doodle's tail feathers had been replaced, the cockerel had briefly  come alive. The first time, he squawked 'Beware!' The second time, he managed to get out the word 'Jack', before becoming metal again.

"I'm sure it was something about Jack Frost," Kirsty said thoughtfully. "But what?"

"Maybe we'll find out if we find another feather, and Doodle speaks to us again!" Rachel suggested. The girls went into the kitchen. Mr Tate was laying the table, and Kirsty's mum was making toast.

"'Morning, you two," said Mr Tate with a smile, as the girls sat down. "What are you planning to do today?"

Before Kirsty or Rachel could answer him, there was a knock at the back door.

"I wonder who that can be!" Mrs Tate said, raising her eyebrows. "It's still quite early."

"I'll get it," said Kirsty, who was nearest.

She opened the door. Outside stood Mr and Mrs Twitching, the Tates' elderly neighbours.

"Oh, Kirsty, good morning," said Mr Twitching. "We're sorry to disturb you, but we were hoping you might have seen Fidget?"

Kirsty frowned, trying to remember. She knew Fidget, the Twitchings' fluffy tabby cat, very well, but she hadn't seen her for the last day or two. "I'm afraid I haven't recently," she replied.

"Oh, dear," Mrs Twitching said, looking upset. "She didn't come home for her dinner last night."

"Come in and ask Mum and Dad," Kirsty suggested, opening the door wider.

"Perhaps they've seen her."

As Mr and Mrs Twitching walked into the kitchen, Kirsty blinked. Just for a moment she thought she'd seen strange wisps of pale smoke, curling and drifting

over the neighbours' heads.

She glanced at Rachel and her parents, but they didn't seem to have noticed anything unusual. Kirsty shook her head. Maybe she was imagining it…

"When was the last time you saw Fidget?" asked Kirsty's mum, as she made cups of tea for the Twitchings.

"Yesterday afternoon," Mrs Twitching replied. "It's very worrying, because she doesn't usually miss a single meal."

"Kirsty and I could help you look for her," suggested Rachel.

"Good idea," Kirsty agreed, finishing off her cereal. "Let's go right away."

"And I'll check our garden and the barn," added Mr Tate.

As Kirsty and Rachel got up from the table, Kirsty stared extra-hard at the Twitchings' heads. She thought she could see wisps of smoke hovering there again, but they were so pale and misty, it was difficult to be sure.

"Rachel," Kirsty said quietly, as they headed outside, "did you notice anything funny about the Twitchings?" Rachel looked puzzled. "What do you mean?"

Kirsty explained about the wisps of smoke. "They were very faint, I'm not sure if I really saw them or not," she finished.

"Do you think they could have been magic?" Rachel asked curiously.

Kirsty felt a thrill of excitement. "Maybe," she said eagerly. "In which case, we'd better keep our eyes open for magic as well as Fidget!"

The girls walked into the village, keeping a sharp look-out for the tabby cat, but there was no sign of her.

"I hope Fidget isn't lost for good," Kirsty said anxiously, staring around her. "Oh!"

Kirsty hadn't been looking where she was going, and she'd bumped into one of the villagers. "I'm so sorry," Kirsty said politely.

The woman glared at her. "Why don't you be more careful?" she said grumpily, and hurried off.

"Well!" gasped Rachel. "That wasn't very nice."

But Kirsty was looking puzzled. "That was Mrs Hill, one of my mum's friends, and she's usually *very* nice," she replied. "I wonder what's wrong?"

Rachel nudged her. "Look over there," she whispered.

Outside the post office, two men were arguing. They both looked very bad-tempered indeed. Then Mrs Burke, who ran the post office, came out to see what was going on. Kirsty was surprised to see that her usually jolly face was downcast.

"There's something funny going on," she whispered to Rachel as they went into the park. "Everybody's in a miserable mood. Look at the children on the swings."

Rachel stared at the children in the playground. They didn't seem to be enjoying their games at all. Every single one of them looked sad and sulky. They didn't even cheer up when the ice-cream van arrived.

The girls stopped at the park gate.

"I think we've been all round Wetherbury.

And there's no sign of Fidget anywhere," Kirsty sighed, glancing at her watch. "We'd better go home, Rachel. It's almost time for lunch."

Rachel nodded. "We can always carry on searching later."

The girls turned back towards the Tates' house. On the way they passed the tiny village cinema. The Saturday morning show had just finished, and the audience was flooding out. Just like everyone else, the people looked glum.

"It must have been a sad film," Rachel whispered to Kirsty.

"But it wasn't," Kirsty replied, frowning. "Look." She pointed at the poster outside the cinema.

"This hilarious film is a must! You'll split your sides laughing!" Rachel read. "Well the audience definitely didn't find it very funny," Rachel pointed out. "Look at their faces."

Kirsty stared at the people trudging gloomily out of the cinema. Suddenly her heart began to pound. There they were again! She could definitely see cloudy smoke drifting over the cinema goers' heads, just as she'd noticed it above her next-door neighbours. "Look, Rachel!" She nudged her friend. "There's that smoke again."

Rachel peered at the people, frowning in concentration. For a moment she thought Kirsty was seeing things. But then she spotted them too – thin, wispy trails of smoke, hovering above the heads of the cinema-goers like little clouds.

"It must be fairy magic!" Rachel said excitedly.

"It could be," Kirsty agreed, her eyes lighting up. "We could be on the trail of another magic feather!"

The girls hurried home. When they entered the house, the first thing they noticed were the clouds hovering over Mr and Mrs Tate!

"Did you find Fidget?" asked Kirsty's mum, who was sitting on the sofa, reading a book. The little white cloud above her head was touched with pink, like a sunset cloud.

"No," Kirsty replied, staring at the grey cloud which was over her dad.

"Oh, dear," Mr Tate said, looking sad.

"I think the goblin with the magic Cloud Feather is close by," Rachel whispered to Kirsty as they ate their sandwiches.

Kirsty nodded. "After lunch, let's go up to my bedroom and plan our next move," she said. "These clouds are beginning to worry me."

"Me, too," Rachel agreed.

As soon as they'd finished their food, the girls ran upstairs. Kirsty threw open her bedroom door.

"Hello!" called a tiny, silvery voice. "I thought you were never coming!"

There, sitting on the windowsill and swinging her legs, sat Pearl the Cloud Fairy.

Goblin Hunting

Pearl was resting her chin on her hands, and she too looked fed up. She wore a beautiful, floaty pink and white dress with a full skirt, and in her hand, she held a pretty pink wand. The wand had a fluffy white tip, from which little pink and white sunset clouds constantly drifted and swirled.

To Kirsty's amazement, a tiny grey cloud hovered over Pearl's head. "Oh, Pearl! You've got a raincloud, too!" Kirsty burst out.

"I know," Pearl sighed. Then her eyes flashed with annoyance. "It's because one of those nasty goblins is using the magic Cloud Feather – and he's doing it all wrong!" she snapped.

"We think the goblin must be very nearby, because everyone in Wetherbury seems to have a cloud over them," Rachel told Pearl.

"I'm sure you're right," Pearl said firmly. "This is definitely fairy magic, which means that mean old goblin can't be far away!" She fluttered restlessly up into the air, leaving a trail of shining pink and white clouds behind her. "Even you two are beginning to get clouds now!" she added.

The girls rushed over to the mirror to look. Sure enough, tiny grey wisps of smoke were beginning to form above their heads.

"Shall we go and find the Cloud Feather?" Kirsty asked eagerly.

Pearl and Rachel both cheered up at that suggestion. Pearl zoomed over to hide herself in Rachel's jacket pocket. Then they all went out into the village.

This time, Rachel and Kirsty could see the clouds over people's heads much more clearly. Some were a pretty pink or orange colour, like sunset clouds, and the people underneath them seemed quiet and dreamy.

Other clouds were black and stormy and the people under those looked gloomy and irritable. Some clouds were drizzling tiny raindrops, making their people look very sad. And a few, very angry people, had clouds shooting little lightning bolts over their heads. "Look." Rachel nudged Kirsty as a man with a lightning cloud hurried past, scowling. "His hair's standing on end like he's had an electric shock!"

"Pearl," Kirsty whispered. "Why hasn't anyone else noticed the clouds?"

Pearl popped her head out of Rachel's pocket. "Only magic beings like fairies can see them," she replied. "And you two, because you're our friends."

"They're getting bigger," said Rachel, staring at a woman who had just passed by with an enormous raincloud above her head.

"We must be getting closer to the feather!" Pearl said eagerly.

"But where can it be?" Kirsty wondered. "We're almost out of the village now." She stopped and looked around. Suddenly she gasped, and pointed at a building to their left.

"Look at the sweet factory!"

The sweet factory stood right on the edge of Wetherbury. A stream of small pink and white clouds were puffing their way out of the tall brick chimney.

"The goblin must be hiding inside the factory," Pearl cried, whizzing out of Rachel's pocket and fluttering up into the air. "It's time to rescue the Cloud Feather!"

A Sticky Situation

"Come on," Rachel said. "Let's go inside."

The girls and Pearl rushed over to the door. But their hearts sank as they saw the large, heavy padlock.

"Of course, it's Saturday. The factory's closed." Kirsty said, looking disappointed. "What are we going to do?"

They stood and thought for a moment. Then Rachel glanced up and a smile spread across her face. "Look!" she said, pointing. "There's an air vent near the roof. We've got our magic fairy dust. Let's turn ourselves into fairies. Then we can all fly in through the air vent."

The Fairy Queen had given Kirsty and Rachel gold lockets full of fairy dust, which they could use to turn themselves into fairies, and back, whenever they needed to.

"Good idea!" Pearl laughed, clapping her hands in delight.

Quickly, Rachel and
Kirsty opened their
lockets, and
sprinkled a little
fairy dust over
themselves. Almost
immediately they
began to shrink,
and beautiful
shimmering fairy wings
grew and unfurled on their backs.

"Come on," Pearl cried, whizzing about
impatiently. "Up we go!" And she flew up
to the air vent in the wall.

Kirsty and Rachel flew after her. Pearl
slipped through first, and the two girls
followed. They all stopped just inside, and
gazed around the factory.

"Wow!" Kirsty breathed, her eyes wide.

Lots of big silver machines were busy making all sorts of different sweets. Stripy humbugs poured out of one machine, while long strings of strawberry liquorice were being piped out of another. Bright yellow sherbert fizzed into paper tubes, and pink and white marshmallows bounced along a moving conveyor-belt.

Chocolate bars were being wrapped in gold foil, while a different machine wrapped toffees in shiny silver paper. There were large sticky lollipops, striped candy canes and boiled sweets in every kind of colour and flavour.

"Isn't this amazing?" said Rachel. "Look at all the different sweets!"

Kirsty looked puzzled. "But surely the people who work here wouldn't have gone home leaving all the machines on?" she pointed out.

Pearl grinned. "I expect they turned them OFF, but somebody else has turned them ON, again."

"The goblin!" Kirsty exclaimed. "Where is he?"

"Let's split up, and see if we can spot him," Pearl replied.

They fluttered off to different parts of the factory. Rachel flew towards a machine which was hard at work mixing fluffy pink candyfloss in a huge silver tub.

She hovered over the machine for a
moment and was about to fly on, when
she heard the sound of someone loudly
smacking their lips.

Rachel flew down to
take a closer look.
There, lying with
his back to her,
on a huge, fluffy
pink cloud beside
the candyfloss
machine, was the
goblin! He was
greedily scooping up
sticky handfuls of candyfloss
from the silver tub, and munching them
happily. He was quite big and round
– probably from stuffing himself with so
much candyfloss, Rachel thought.

She flew a little nearer and peeped over the goblin's shoulder, to see if she could spy the magic Cloud Feather. There it was – pearly-grey and shimmering in his hand. Tiny pink and white clouds drifted from it, as the goblin waved it about.

I must tell Pearl and Kirsty, Rachel thought. She turned to fly off, but as she did so, one wing brushed the goblin's shoulder. With a roar of surprise, the goblin reached up and grabbed Rachel tightly.

"You're not having my feather!" he shouted, and stuffed Rachel inside one of the pink clouds which were drifting past.

Poor Rachel was trapped. She tried to push her way out of the cloud, but she couldn't make a hole in it. The cloud drifted up and away from the goblin.

"Kirsty! Pearl!" Rachel called as loudly as she could. "HELP!"

Kirsty heard her friend's voice. She turned, and saw the cloud with Rachel inside, floating past the marshmallow machine. To Kirsty's horror, it was heading straight towards the factory's tall chimney.

"Oh, no!" Kirsty gasped. "If that cloud floats up the chimney, we'll never get Rachel back!"

Candyfloss Clouds

Quickly, Pearl flew over to Kirsty. "Which cloud is Rachel in?" she asked.

"That one..." Kirsty began, pointing. Then she stopped. There were so many clouds floating around, she'd lost sight of Rachel. "Oh, I don't know, Pearl. That goblin!" she went on crossly, "I've got a few things to say

to him! Can you make me
human-sized again?"

Pearl nodded. "Don't worry," she
said, "I'll find Rachel. You get the
feather."

With a wave of her wand, she
zapped Kirsty back up to her
normal size. Then she
flew off to search
through the clouds.
Kirsty stormed
angrily over to
the goblin. She was
usually scared of the nasty
creatures – especially since Jack Frost
had used his magic to make them
bigger. But Kirsty was so annoyed, she
didn't care. Rachel might be in danger,
and it was all the goblin's fault.

The goblin was lying on top of his fluffy cloud, still eating candyfloss. When he saw Kirsty marching towards him, he looked nervous. Quickly, he stuffed the Cloud Feather into his mouth out of sight.

"Give me that feather!" Kirsty demanded.

"Wha' fe'er?" the goblin spluttered, trying to keep his mouth closed.

Kirsty frowned. How was she going to get the feather out of the goblin's mouth?

She spotted a candyfloss stick lying on

the floor. That gave her an idea. She picked it up, and began tickling the goblin on the soles of his leathery feet!

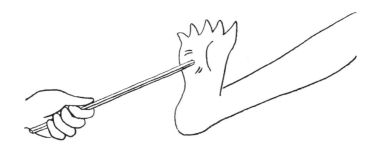

The goblin began to chuckle, but he kept his mouth shut. "Shtop it," he mumbled. But then he couldn't hold his laughter in any longer. "Oh, ha ha ha," he guffawed. And as his laughter burst out, so did the magic Cloud Feather!

Kirsty made a grab for it, but the

goblin was quicker.
"Oh, no!" he
grinned, snatching
the feather away.
"This is *my* feather!
I'm the only one who
knows how to make
it work."

"Actually, I know how to make it
work too!" called a silvery voice.

Kirsty turned to see Pearl flying
towards them. To Kirsty's relief, she
was towing a pink cloud behind her
with Rachel inside.

Rachel's head was sticking out of a hole in the cloud, and she grinned at Kirsty. "Hey, this cloud's made of candyfloss!" she called. "And it's delicious. I can eat my way out!" And she took another bite.

Pearl flew down to Kirsty and the goblin. "I can make the clouds do all sorts of things," she went on. "They will float exactly where I tell them to. I can even make them dance around me." She held out her hand to the goblin. "Why don't you give me the feather and let me show you?"

The goblin looked sly. "No, it's mine!" he said. "Anyway, I can do those tricks myself."

"Go on, then," Pearl challenged.

The goblin frowned in a huge effort of concentration. He began waving the feather around. Very slowly all the clouds in the room drifted towards him. He twiddled the feather, and the clouds began to whirl around him in a circle, faster and faster. "See?" the goblin boasted.

"OK, you know what to do, Rachel," Pearl whispered to her.

Pearl let go of Rachel's candyfloss cloud, and she and Kirsty watched as it sailed over to the goblin. Rachel's cloud began to whizz around him along with the others. It got nearer and nearer to the goblin. Then, suddenly, as her cloud sped past the goblin's hand, Rachel stuck her arm out of the hole and seized the Cloud Feather!

A Silver Lining

"Give that back!" the goblin shouted. Every time Rachel's cloud flew past him, he tried to recapture the feather, but missed.

The clouds were whizzing round so fast now that Rachel was feeling very dizzy. "Help!" she called. "Somebody stop this cloud!"

Pearl swooped down and deftly
plucked the feather out of
Rachel's hand. Then she
waved it expertly a
few times, and the
clouds began to
slow down and
drift away.

Kirsty caught
hold of Rachel's
cloud, and
pulled it
open to free
her friend.

Rachel tumbled
out, dizzily. The
goblin was dizzy too,
from all the clouds
whirling round his head.

He was staggering around in circles, looking for the Cloud Feather. When he saw that Pearl had it, he lurched forward and made a clumsy grab for the little fairy. Pearl darted out of the way just in time, but the goblin lost his balance. He tumbled over, and fell head-first into the toffee-wrapping machine!

The girls and Pearl watched in amazement as the yelling goblin was wrapped in a huge sheet of shiny silver paper. Then the goblin-shaped toffee was shunted along the conveyor-belt, boxed and gift-wrapped with a sparkly silver ribbon.

"That serves him right!" Rachel laughed.

"Come on," grinned Pearl. "Let's get out of here before he unwraps himself!"

Kirsty sprinkled herself with fairy dust and immediately turned into a fairy again. Then the three friends flew out of the factory through the air vent. Outside, Pearl waved her magic wand and returned the girls to their normal size.

"And I'd better make sure everyone in Wetherbury gets back to normal right away!" Pearl laughed.

She waved the feather in an intricate pattern through the air. "That should do it," she declared cheerfully. They set off back to the Tates' house, with Pearl hiding in Rachel's pocket again.

"Look," whispered Rachel, as they made their way through the village. "No one has a cloud over their head anymore!"

"And everyone's happy and laughing again," added Kirsty. The children playing in the park were all smiles now, and as the girls passed the post office, Mrs Burke gave them a cheery wave.

"I'll give Doodle his beautiful Cloud Feather back," Pearl said, when they arrived at the Tates' house. "He'll be so pleased to see it!"

Rachel and Kirsty stood in the garden, and watched happily as Pearl flew up to the top of the barn. The fairy replaced the Cloud Feather in Doodle's tail. A moment later, the cockerel's fiery feathers began to sparkle with fairy magic.

"Doodle's coming to life again!" Kirsty cried. "Listen hard, Rachel!"

Doodle's magnificent feathers shimmered in the sun. "Frost w—!" he squawked. But the next moment, he was cold, hard metal again.

"Beware, Jack Frost w—" Kirsty said thoughtfully, as Pearl flew down to join them. "What does it mean?"

"I don't know," replied Pearl. "But be careful. Jack Frost won't want to lose any more magic feathers! And now I must return to Fairyland."

The pretty fairy hugged Rachel and Kirsty, scattering little, shiny pink and white clouds around them. Then she fluttered up into the sky. "Goodbye!" she called, "And good luck in finding the other four weather feathers!"

"Goodbye!" called Kirsty and Rachel, waving.

Smiling, Pearl waved her wand at them and disappeared into the clouds.

The girls went into the house, where Mr and Mrs Tate were in the living-room watching TV.

"Oh, Kirsty, Rachel, here you are at last," said Mrs Tate, jumping to her feet. "The Twitchings phoned a little while ago, and invited us over for tea."

"And they said they've got some good news for us," Mr Tate added.

Kirsty and Rachel looked at each other.

"They must have found Fidget!" Kirsty exclaimed happily.

The girls hurried
next-door with
Mr and Mrs Tate.

Mr Twitching
opened the door,
a big smile on
his face. "Come
in," he said.
"We've got a
surprise for you!"

He led them into the
living-room, where Mrs Twitching
was kneeling on the rug next to a cat
basket. A big, fluffy tabby cat was
curled up inside.

"She's been a very busy girl," Mrs
Twitching said proudly. "Look!"

There in the basket were three tiny
kittens, snuggled up close to their mum.

Two were tabby like Fidget, and one was black with a little white spot on the top of its head. They were so young, their eyes were still closed.

"Oh, Rachel, aren't they gorgeous!" Kirsty breathed, stroking the black and white kitten gently on its tiny head.

"We'll be looking for good homes for them when they're bigger," said Mr Twitching. "But they can't leave their mum for eight or nine weeks."

"Oh!" Kirsty gasped, her eyes shining. "Maybe I could have one?"

"I don't see why not," Mrs Tate said, smiling.

"Which one would you like, Kirsty?" Mrs Twitching asked.

"This one," Kirsty said, stroking the black and white kitten again. It yawned sleepily.

"And I know the perfect name for her," Rachel said, smiling at her friend. "You can call her Pearl!"

FERN THE GREEN FAIRY
1-84362-019-7

SAFFRON THE YELLOW FAIRY
1-84362-018-9

AMBER THE ORANGE FAIRY
1-84362-017-0

RUBY THE RED FAIRY
1-84362-016-2

HEATHER THE VIOLET FAIRY
1-84362-022-7

IZZY THE INDIGO FAIRY
1-84362-021-9

SKY THE BLUE FAIRY
1-84362-020-0

The Weather Fairies

GOLDIE THE SUNSHINE FAIRY
1-84362-641-1

PEARL THE CLOUD FAIRY
1-84362-635-7

ABIGAIL THE BREEZE FAIRY
1-84362-634-9

CRYSTAL THE SNOW FAIRY
1-84362-633-0

HAYLEY THE RAIN FAIRY
1-84362-638-1

STORM THE LIGHTNING FAIRY
1-84362-637-3

EVIE THE MIST FAIRY
1-84362-636-5

Collect all of the Rainbow Magic books!

by Daisy Meadows

Win a Rainbow Magic Sparkly T-Shirt and Goody Bag!

In every book in the Rainbow Magic Weather series (books 8-14) there is a hidden picture of a magic feather with a secret letter in it. Find all seven letters and re-arrange them to make a special Fairyland word, then send it to us. Each month we will put the entries into a draw. The winner will receive a Rainbow Magic Sparkly T-shirt and Goody Bag!

Send your entry on a postcard to Rainbow Magic Competition, Orchard Books, 96 Leonard Street, London EC2A 4XD. Australian readers should write to 32/45-51 Huntley Street, Alexandria, NSW 2015. Don't forget to include your name and address.